T0165349

Above the Drama

A FICTIONAL NOVEL

WRITTEN BY

NEFERTITI BROWN

Order this book online at www.trafford.com
or email orders@trafford.com

Most Trafford titles are also available at major online book retailers.

© Copyright 2011 Nefertiti Brown.
All rights reserved. No part of this publication may be reproduced, stored in a retrieval
system, or transmitted, in any form or by any means, electronic, mechanical, photocopying,
recording, or otherwise, without the written prior permission of the author.

Printed in the United States of America.

ISBN: 978-1-4269-8261-3 (sc)
ISBN: 978-1-4269-8262-0 (e)

Trafford rev. 08/11/2011

www.trafford.com

North America & international
toll-free: 1 888 232 4444 (USA & Canada)
phone: 250 383 6864 ♦ fax: 812 355 4082

ACKNOWLEDGMENTS

Special thanks to my supportive family,

Ms. Dana Blowstien, Ms S. Holliday and **Ms L Edwards**

These named people have been the inspiration and back
bone of this project and many novels to follow.
Persevere don't ever give up on your dreams,

And a very special thanks to

Charisse M. White

of Belladonna Reese Photography Production

TABLE OF CONTENTS

"I want to take you on a journey down memory lane back when we lived on Saint Thomas Drive summer of 1995. We lived through or ups and downs, but above all we always had love

Above
the
Drama."

Chapter 1

Meeting the Family

FAMILY CRISIS

"*R*ing, Ring, Ring? Hello, I answered with sleep in my voice, it's only 12pm I thought to myself. "Shit, I don't get up till 2:00pm!" Rashidah ain't here, who dis calling so early anyways I yelled? It's A-Boogie, ok ... whatever bye! I slammed the phone down and turned over to go back to sleep. Seems like seconds later, I hear my name being repeated as if there was a scratched record left playing on the record player. "Symirah! Symirah! you better get down here right now," yelled my mother Basimah. We jokingly called her Big Bas when we're out of her sight. Ma, I'm coming I have to put some clothes on. Well you better make it fast Symirah, its time for a family meeting. As I stormed down the stairs, I

3

see everyone sitting at the big round table, which included Rashidah my younger sister, LaQuan my oldest brother and Malik my middle brother. I knew this was a serious family affair. My little brother Raheem was home from military school to attend this meeting, so that says it all. You see my parents strive on excellence. They believed that if school wasn't your option, then you had to work.

I took my seat and my mother started the meeting right away. First off, I want to say that everyone at this table represents the Coleman Family, and everything you do reflects on our reputation as a whole. Then my father RaQuan interrupted saying, "usually mom out talks us all." I was in a state of shock, when my dad started to speak. Your mother has informed me that there is a new found love going on between one of my princesses. Remember that I don't play when it comes to one of my girls and if this young man wants to talk to my girl he has to see your mother and I first. Symirah looked shocked to find out her parents knew about her secret love.

So Symirah, when do we meet this young man father asked. MMMM..... stumbling over her words Symirah said, "u mm Oh yeah, tonight I will invite him to dinner Dad if it's ok?" RaQuan said "sure, Invite the man over princess," we all can sit down at the table to eat tonight. Symirah asked to be excused from the family meeting to call her baby and invite him over for dinner at the house. Symirah rushed upstairs smiling from ear to ear, grabbed the phone and called Rodger. Hey Baby with a smiling voice, I want you to come to dinner tonight at my house. "Oh yeah sure," Rodger said with a smiling voice, "what time?" Symirah replied, "Umm about 5:00PM."

Ok love? I will be there. One more thing, I love you Symirah. Love you too Baby. See you tonight. Later. Bye. You know raising children in the hood was hard enough, but we were determined to raise our children with good morals. RaQuan had his own Street investigation going on with Mr. Rodger Morgan. You see, RaQuan was from the streets, but he changed his life when he met and married Basimah. They made a promise to each other never to look back once they left the streets. They also vowed to raise their children with good family ethics, love, respect, prayer, and to keep a good family was the key. Mr. Morgan had his own plan already in place since the day he met Symirah.

Rodger made it very clear to Symirah that they could never tell her family about his past. His very words were: What is done in the past stays in the past. We are living for the future, and I want to build my future with you Symirah. Oh, those words just made Symirah melt. Being swept off her feet by this man twice her age was such a thrill. Mr. Rodger was much smarter and more experienced then Symirah, and he was planning to get as many girls under his belt to complete his mission. When Rodger hung up the phone with Symirah, he called his baby mamma just to assure her he was coming over but he would be a little late tonight.

Dam, I got this shit on lock with all these girls, Rodger thought to himself. I got my baby mamma, Ciara and Symirah and I ain't letting none of them go, he thougt to himself. I love being a kept man. All my girls will pay my bills, keep my cell phone on, feed me, and dress me. Shit, they pay my rent and don't live with me, what more can a man ask for. I should have thought of this before I went to jail and did 10years. These girls are more gullible then I thought, just real easy like. Now I gotta impress this family, so I'm gonna put on my best performance yet. Smiling and snickering to myself, as I begin to get dressed; Symirah is my gold mine, I can't fuck this one up.

Dear Diary,   *August 7, 1995*

I am so afraid of my Dad and Rodger meeting I hope the personalities don't clash it has been two days since I met Rodger Morgan and it was love at first sight. I love this man and I pray all goes well when the family meets my man until next time............

Dinner With The New Boyfriend

Yelling as I always do, Ma where is my lipstick at? I have to look good before Rodger gets here. Ask your sister, my mother replied, I have no clue where it is. Ok, Symirah called out, Rashidah, have you seen my MAC Lipstick. "Rashidah yelled girl, I 'm so sorry I had it, remember I had a date with A-Boogie." Wow, you always using my stuff. Sucking my teeth, anyway. Raheem make sure you seat Rodger, before I make my grand entrance. Raheem yelled, "don't worry I have my own set of questions to ask this man, I can't come home without my sisters to bother that is gonna make me mad." Please everyone get to know him before you push him under the bus. "Ding Dong". "Oh no, that is him now"; I got to go put on my clothes. Someone please answer the door! "Of course," my father answered the door. Hello young man, how can I help you? Hello my name is Rodger. RaQuan stated, "Oh Yes Rodger come in, we have heard very little about you. Looking shocked, Rodger replied, really!" We'll sit the dining table and Symirah will be down in a few. Just take a seat. Thank you Mr. Coleman for having me over for dinner. Meanwhile Symirah and Rashidah were upstairs talking. Girl, I'm getting so nervous, I hope Dad and Raheem don't tear Rodger apart with their questions Rashidah. Yeah girl, you remember when daddy first met your man A-Boogie Rashidah. Oh yeah, right! And that's what I am afraid of laughing loudly. "Girls, let's go get down stairs your diner is getting cold!" Big Bas yelled loudly. We're coming Ma both girls yelled in unison. The girls finally made it to the table still snickering all the way to their seats, after the laughter ceased there was silence around the whole table. The silence was broken by my youngest brother Raheem.

Wow Rodger man, you look as old as my dad! Now how old did you say you were? LaQuan agreed with his little brother with a node of his head. Rodger replied, "26 little brother." Raheem looked at him with a mean stare and said, "I really think you're up to something, because you're moving too quick with my sister." I have my eye on you man, as Raheem shook his head in disgrace. "Negative," Rodger answered; man is this going to be twenty questions? I did not sign up for this. Are we having dinner? My father looked up at Rodger, as if he wanted to choke him for his disrespectful remark. Hey, let's all just eat shall we.

RaQuan politely grunted, it took everything in him not to punch Rodger in his face for taking to his son like that. I had to say something to break the tension, and change the mood. So young man, what are your intentions with my princess? Well sir, I love Symirah and I want to take her hand in marriage, if that is alright with the family? Hold on Rodger, you don't even know my princess. And I just heard about you a few days ago! What do you mean you love her, and you want to take her hand in marriage? You working? You're too old for her, and you have lived half your life. It ain't no way you are telling me your 26, cause game recognize game. Looks to me your 40 something right?

Now you starting off by lying in my face? Rodger began to choke and hold his head down. Sir let me correct myself. Did I say 26? Well I meant 46,.... Stuttering but age is just a number. And to answer your question, before I am a motivational speaker to the young men in the community. That is how I make my living, and it is a paid position Mr. Coleman. Now sir with all due respect, I am in love with Symirah and I am going to marry her. I was really hoping to have your blessing along with the family, before we made arrangements to get married in two weeks. As the conversation went on, Symirah stared off and began to day dream at the table just thinking back....Two days before that is as far as she could remember. Symirah was on the porch just chilling with her girls, and this fine ass man walked by we connected with our eyes. And my heart went wild. Shit, it wasn't like I knew this man was dating my best friend. We told each other secrets, but she never told me this one. Ciara and I been best friends, since we were born. "Hey boo," Ciara said to the man that was walking down the street. "What's up shorty," he replied as he grabbed her and they engaged in a kiss. I was so mad, but I didn't know why I was acting like this over a man that ain't mine. I was trying to act as if I could care less. But best friends know each other. Ciara looked at me and said, "girl what's wrong?" Nothing, I just don't fell too good.

I'm going to go lay down. Ciara said "Ok, I will see you tomorrow." Ok, later. Little did she know Rodger slipped me his number while they were kissing. "Yes, it's on tonight!" With his fine ass.

I had to get away, because I could not bear to see my man kissing that ghetto girl. I had to talk to someone who wouldn't judge me so I called my cousin Haneefah. "Ring!" "Ring!" Hello, Hey girl, I hope you're not busy I really need to talk. What's up Symirah? Well, you know me and Ciara are best friends right? Yes, I know so what about it.

I really want to take her man, because she has no skills with keeping him happy, like I do. Now Symirah, skills? You know its gonna be drama. So you need to look at the whole picture and see both sides, before you go jumping into this thing off some bull shit. Symirah said with a sinister grin, "well he looks good and I am calling him tonight to see what is up." What do you mean you calling him tonight? You have is number Mira? You had to see the way he was looking at me while kissing Ciara. Wow, Mira you fell for that old trick! Girl... um, I thought you we smarter than that being my older cousin and all. What? Listen Haneefah this man really likes me. Besides, I look better than Ciara.

He took one look at me and now he's my man, so she can kiss that one goodbye. I get what I want, remember I'm always daddy's little princess. "Ok," Haneefah said with sadness in her voice. Mira, this is not the time to fight with you, but I want you to know that you should always think with your head and not your heart. I'll talk to you later, be careful. Yeah, yeah, yeah... Haneefah, whatever smacking her lips in anger saying, "you know you gonna be on edge for all my juicy gossip later, Bye." Back at the diner table, I hear my name being called. Hello! Symirah, hey Symirah stop dreaming! Oh, I said as I snapped out of my dream trying to get it together. Yes, I finally answered, are you alright baby Basimah said?

Yeah Ma, I just haven't been feeling my best lately. I really need to go a lay down now. Raheem make sure your sister gets to her room. Man, I am... What did you say? Nothing dad. Raheem got up and grabbed his sister by the arm. Come on Mira, let's move it. I need to get back to my food. Symirah cried loudly, can Rodger come too? Symirah, now you know no outsider can walk all over my home. Rodger was just leaving right? Uh mm yes, yes Sir I am. I have to prepare my speech for tomorrow. I love you Symirah he yelled loudly. Love you too babe, good night. RaQuan followed behind Roger and whispered in his ear over my dead body; you're too old for my daughter, and got in his car speeding away angry down the street.

Little did the family know, RaQuan was going to a meeting on the east side of town. No one knew how Rodger was very clever and charming. He uses his bedroom skills to lure women in. Rodger thought that young girls always fall victim to the MD, once you have control of their minds, it's very easy for everything else to fall in line. Power over the mind is dangerous, if a negative person is able to control you because your mind is centro-control unit of the human being, so man thinks he shall be.

Before I could get to my room I forgot I left my diary on the hallway on the table. I just had to continue where I left off I was overwhelmed with joy.

Dear Diary part II   *August 7, 1995*
I could not wait to get to my room so I could write down how impressed I was to see Rodger..... stand up to my dad and brothers. He is such a strong man and that turns me on. I can't wait to marry him and have his baby. I hope his first child will be a son you know a little Rodger lol until next time......

The Cat Fight Between Best Friends

As I entered my room, I noticed my window was opened so I shut it and to my surprise Ciara was standing behind me. Ciara shouted, "what's up Symirah!" What are you doing in my house? Symirah replied. Well, first of all you don't answer my calls no more, and I wanted to know if what people are saying in the streets is true. What is that Ciara? That you fucking my man! Your man? Hold on little girl if he was yours then why you can't keep him satisfied? Ciara said quickly with assurance. I please my man that is why he is at my house now! Really, so why would he be in my house eating with my family tonight, if he was your man?

No, he was not he has been with me all day. Well I know you better stay far away from my man, because I'm not playing with you Symirah. What? Little girl are you talking shit in my house. And Symirah moved closer and started to reach for Ciara's neck. Rashidah started yelling loudly stop; please stop, "Mira she ain't worth it." Rashidah knew her big sister was going to kill her, after the things Rodger said at dinner tonight. Ma! Ma! please help me Symirah and Ciara are fighting. By the time Rashidah could get her words out clearly, Symirah was on top of Ciara punching her in the face repetitively.

Blood was everywhere Basimah ran in a panic up the stairs LaQuan and Malik grabbed Symirah by both arms off of Ciara, and began to drag her into the other room. What are you girls fighting over. Ladies don't fight, animals do. And how did you get in this house young lady? As Ciara begin to pull herself slowly up off the floor, Rashidah asked again how you got in the house. Ciara answered, "I climbed through the open window." Well, I hope my dad didn't hear this cause you know what will happen if he finds out. Give Mira this message, it ain't over bitch. "Oh, yes it is over and get the hell out of my house, before we all trash you."

Basimah yelled! Ciara ran down the stairs, she knew that Rashidah and he mom was serious. The Coleman family was known for destroying you. And, what I did coming in their home without an invite I was wrong, but I was blinded by my love for Rodger. "She will never have my man, Ciara angrily shouted with a teary voice and a bloody nose. I put everything including my life on this, that bitch is as good as dead. Hey Sis! Girl, that Ciara is crazy sneaking in our house like that. She sure is, don't she know we family and if I fight, we all fight. "Now settle down girls," Basimah stated, we can't let your dad know what just happened, so let's keep this quiet. I don't want to make him angry.

He has enough to worry about since you want to get married and all. Remember, we all have to do our part to keep this family's good name. We don't let evil people take us out of our own self-respect. Now Symirah, you need to change your people, places and things, before this gets out. Symirah stated, "I know what to do Ma, and don't worry I will be more careful." I just don't understand how two best friends can be at each others throat like this. Ma, you know she thinks I took her man right? Well did you? No, I had answer with my mouth, but I knew in my heart it was true I took her man. Anyway, he was never her man, if he was looking my way.

Well, the rule of code is never to date or flirt with your friends, or relatives' man in that way. Oh wow, Ma that is real old school, is that from your time? In today's time, our world it is if he is feeling me and I am feeling him, we get up

together; whatever happens, it will happen right Rashidah?
Yes sis, that is what normally happens.

Dear Diary continuation.......
*Can't believe my best-friend, that I grew up with
came at me ova a man that ain't even her man
uh. If she thinks I am sleeping on her she has lost
her mind. Over, hmm she thinks it's over no it
has just begun her threats are harmless for I am
the truth! She better be watching her own back. I
got my little crew on lock and I can and set it off.
I got to make this call, then we will see who is the
truth! Until the next time.......*

CHAPTER 2

THE EAST SIDE

RaQuans Meeting on the East Side

Now after my Street investigation, I found out Rodger Morgan was the leader of (Money & Bitches) The MB Crew, a street rival crew on the west side of town. RaQuan did not like what they stood for, nor did he want his little girl with anyone associated with this wild bunch. RaQuan was making his own plans. He had put away his old ways to be a good role model to his family, and now this Rodger Morgan is trying to take one of my princesses out of my life.

"I am going to get down to the bottom of this," RaQuan screamed loudly. Why, Why my little girl? He can't take care of her like I do? RaQuan sat in his car and sat he thought for a while, before making his call to Madd Dog and the RGG Crew. Yeah you know what's up;Uh, Ok we all know where to meet lets come out of retirement for the blood brother's love. I was the first to arrive at Devils Peak on the east side of town. I had so many mixed feelings about this gathering of The Old G's. I knew once we met at this point it was no looking back. It was serious business. T- Mac pulled up in his BMW 740mxl and on the passenger side was Madd Dog. Looks like RGG has reunited its crew to complete one last mission.

Yeah man, remember we used to get it in, and the work we put in....man these young cats don't know what it is. As they all laughed simultaneously, RaQuan had a serious face the entire time. Wow Madd Dog, man I knew once I called you things were going to get serious. This MB Crew leader is really crawling under my skin lying and brainwashing my little girl Symirah. Man, I need you to handle this for me. I promised Basimah that I would not look back for her and the kids. I have to be the example and head of my family. Well, Rah you know whatever I do, I do it big and I leave it clean, spotless. Now you done called me out of retirement, it's on. Madd Dog replied. I know, that's why I called you, so the job will get done.

I'm on it Rah, no need to worry, I owe you one. What Madd Dog? Yeah man, I owe you for holding my people down, when

I was in Kingston Prison for 10yrs. Because of that, this is my gift to you and your family. This day will be kept between blood brothers. Rah stated, in unison till death, we depart. Word Madd Dog, word up, Rah. That's what's up T-Mac was never big on words, but this time I knew something was eating at him as I looked his way he said, "blood is thicker than water, we are united by blood." "Ok man, later," smiling with my head held high." I knew that my troubles were over. Later man, I got to get back to my family. You know how we do, gotta keep my woman happy Raquan said, in his smiling voice.

One love, yeah RGG peace. As I'm driving back home, my phone rings and it is Basimah asking my were a bouts. Yes, babe I had to go fill up the truck, so you don't have to stop on your way to work in the morning. Basimah shouted loudly, "now girls, this is the kinda man you want to select." A real man that thinks about you, although you're not with him and has your best interest at heart. Honey, see you when you get back, I love you more. As I hung up the phone I heard,... Aww, looks like the two love birds are at it again; whew, yuck get a room. We laughed hysterically, till we rolled off the bed onto the floor. Now, before you lose your composure. Wow, Ma using big words ha.. ha.. ha.. ha.....

Now, just one minute girls on a serious tip. Drum roll, Ma is getting serious, this may take a while. As I was saying silly little girls, we as women must know our worth. This is the key to self-respect. Yes, Ma and as we respect ourselves, no one can come in and disrespect us. For we are bold, virtuous women that were created by God for one strong man. Yes, yes girls, I am so glad you have not forgotten. Well goodnight now get your beauty sleep. Simultaneously, we shouted goodnight Big Bas. As we laughed out loud, mom closed the door shut.

"Rashidah!" Symirah whispered, in a sleepy voice Rashidah replied, "what is it now!" You and A-Boogie been dating for a long time, but marriage is not an option I see. "Symirah, "Symirah, in my relationship we are taking our time to know each other well. Marriage is a full time commitment we're not ready to take. "Symirah, are you getting cold feet? "Symirah replied, a little bit, but it seems like I have known Rodger all my life. Rashidah, we finish each others sentences, we think alike, and he understands that I am a virgin. Rodger respects my body. Symirah, girl you haven't known him long enough, to know whether he respects you or not. Remember you chose the man, he doesn't choose you. Getting out of relationships are easy. "How is it easy Rashidah?" Symirah honey, you can just leave. It's that easy. Rashidah you maybe right, but I ain't leaving Rodger and his fine ass sorry; Rodger just does it for me. Goodnight Symirah mumbled as she rolled over to grab her book.

Dear Diary,

Seems like we have more to talk about. My sister is young and doesn't understand when love comes around you have to hold on to it tight, and never let go. True love doesn't take years to grow. I can't give up on Rodger, that is hard to do. I am going to get close as I can to him. Until next time.....

PILLOW TALK BETWEEN LOVERS

RaQuan, can you answer my question truthfully? Basimah whispered to him softly. As she begin to nibble on his neck. Your gonna start something in here tonight, if you keep that up honey. What? This... Now, how do I answer the question, little tiger. Ok now what was the question as I laughed as quietly as possible. Of course,now what is this question and why all the serious tones in your voice. Well, I have been dreaming these aweful nightmares lately of you getting killed in a shoot-out with another gang. As tears rolled down her eyes and her voice became shaky.

I know that it is just a dream because you left those guns along many years ago, but I am afraid and I can't stop dreaming this same dream. I really did not what him to find out what happened tonight with the girls, so I had to place his mind on other things. Basimah babe, the promise I made to you and my family I won't look back and pick up my guns again. "I can't believe I just lied to my wife. We are always honest to each other." I am glad it's dark in our room. I thought to myself. I enjoy these moments together, and I can't put the streets before my family. Remember when I was running RRG?

Yes, I remember well, Madd Dog, T- Mac, Mustafa, and all of you running St. Thomas Drive. How everyone was afraid of your crew. No one tried to cross your crew. You know back then people had more respect, or at least you made them respect you. Ha, ha...babe your too funny. We just had an understanding, that the people we liked could stay in the neighborhood and others had to move or get robbed every day. Yeah a bunch of gang bangers, I wasn't scared of your gang. Ok, big Bas, I was in love with you, my preacher's daughter who could never come outside after the street lights came on... as they both started laughing loudly. Shush..... we are getting too loud in here.

Alright I may have been in the house but I am smart because of it. Now imagine if I were not keeping my grades up, we would not be able to own our business, be home owners, nor be wealthy. We keep God first, and we stay praying everyday. Ok now, miss Bas there you go, we are not going to be boastful people for God, is a jealous God, but grateful for what God has allowed us to have accomplished in life. Without God this ain't possible. Remember preacher's daughter, you taught me that. So where is your faith? You know Rah, your right. Let's talk later, because these last few days my headaches have been coming back. We don't need all this drama. Bas, we are above the drama, because we have God in us.

Alright, now kiss me goodnight.....

Basimahs Multiple Personalities

Oh, wow here goes those migraines again. First thing, this Morning. Girls, you need to get up we have to get ready for the road trip. Ma, what road trip the girls yelled. I'm not your mother, we go school together I am not that old. I wish everyone would get it together, I am ready to leave. As I approached the door to my surprise, my car was waiting for me. Off I go; I just love road trips. Symirah watched sadly and helplessly out the bedroom window, as her mother drove down the long winding driveway wondering to herself, what personality mom is in now and when will she come back. Wow, Rashidah, we really need mom right now. Yeah, this is not the time. How will we tell Dad this time, we could not stop her. Let's call Dad now, maybe he can help. Hello Devon, I am on my way I hope you cleared your schedule, I need color. Who is this calling? I know you can't be serious this is Carmen and I need this done right away because I am leaving town. What color?... Red duh! You know what I like, but still you ask questions. "I don't pay you to ask me a bunch of questions, Carmen yelled loudly." bursting thru the door of Creations by Devon Unisex. This shop was in the heart of the M& B Crew territory on the west side. Devon just stood still looking at Carmen swiftly walking into his business scaring his clientele.

"Listen Carmen", I will be right with you and could you please lower your voice. I can hear you clearly, Devon asked in a calm mellow tone voice. Finally, Carmen quieted down and had a seat. "Carmen," Devon called, "I am ready to start your hair." Well Devon, I do need the works looks like I have not been here in a while; my nails are all broken and these feet of mine need a total make over. I really hope you are ready for me today. "Well Carmen, if I wasn't I am now. They both laughed. Karen cancel all my appointments for the day, this is an ex-stream emergency. Devon knew she was paid so with her tip, he could make his days work off of

Carmen he thought to himself. Now that is the service I am used to Devon.

And my tip will be worth your while. Hello Dad, Oh daddy in my crying voice mom has gone off in one of her personalities again, and we could not stop her this time. Take it easy girls, I will be home soon my meeting is closing as we speak. Do you know which direction your mother left in. Yeah Dad, down 22nd street and Golden Ave. I promise you girls mom will be home tonight. Promise Dad? I promise. You know Symirah, Dad is a man of his word, mom will come home please stop crying. Rashidah, I can't help but to cry so many thoughts keep rolling in my mind. I don't know which personality has over taken mom.

Dear Diary,   *August 8, 1995*
Now my mom has been having headaches and the personalities have over taken her. I know its because of me bringing a new man in the house. I thought I was following the family rules, were am I going wrong? And please God let mom (Big Bas) be alright. Until next time......

Listen, no matter which one has over taken mom, we must stay positive at all times. Hey, remember the poem mom keep us reciting until we memorized it? Yes.

Well, come on lets repeat it together, it should make things better. Simultaneously, they started to re-sight the poem............

> *"WHAT A WOMAN NEEDS IS A SOUND MIND THAT IS ANCHORED ON A SUPERIREOR BEING. A WOMAN SHOULD BE STRONG IN HER BELEIFS WITH SOUND MORALS AND SELF RESPECT. NOT EASILY PURSUED BY THE MISFOURTUNES OF LIFE, BUT HAVING LONGSUFFERING, PAIENTS AND LOVE TO ENDURE TO THE END.*
>
> *WHILE A VIRTOUS WOMAN WILL BE ONE THAT CAN TAKE CARE OF HOME AND FAMILY. A VIRTOUS WOMAN YES THAT IS ME."*

Feeling better? Yeah, a little. Ok, so let's go to the mall and shop, now that can make a girl feel so much better. Staying in the house waiting for dad will just make us worry more. Rashidah yelled loudly to her brothers, "LaQuan, Malik, we are going out we will be back." Malik answered, "is mom around to take the business calls?" "Mom is out for the day," Symirah answered. LaQuan, you and Malik can handle the phones for a couple of hours, thanks bye.

Off to the mall, the girls giggle all the way to the car. Meanwhile, RaQuan had been driving for hours, and still no sight of Big Bas, he knew he had to keep his word to his daughters. "Looks like I have to call on my crew, "he said as he reached for his cell phone it was ringing already. Hello, yeah its me Madd Dog, just checking in on you, Ra what's good? Aww man, I was just gonna call you I have another problem. What is it? Big Bas is missing, she gone off in one of those personality things again. Man, I should have listened to those doctors, but I thought I could handle this on my own. Bas can be any where, and I don't need the pigs in my business, you feel me. Yeah man, I feel you, so I am on it I am calling the entire crew.

What car did she drive? Looks like the truck. Ok, the suburban? Yeah. Rah man go home and stay with your family. We got this, and I promise Bas will be home tonight. Peace, ok peace. T-Mac knew when to look for Basimah those personalities always lead her to bad places like the West side. Devon, stop talking so much, I have to get going you are prolonging my plans. Well, Miss Carmen had you made an appointment things would have been different. I just have to style you and you will be well on your way. Look, Girl here comes trouble, walking thru the door. What trouble its a gang a old school gang the RRG Crew I think. I don't know any gang members.

Well, Carmen looks like they know you, and they are headed this way. T-Mac said in a quiet voice, "Basimah your hair looks nice, let's go this hood is dangerous." Excuse me but my name is Carmen, I believe you have me wrong. Madd Dog scoped Bas up like a new born baby, while T-Mac took her truck keys and headed for the door. Devon was speechless. Over hearing the conversation, Karen said, "did he just call Carmen Basimah?" I know that was not thee Basimah Coleman? RaQuan's wife? That is a huge problem, because Rodger should have been notified about this visit. Looks like she walked into the wrong shop.

"Oh...Ooo, Rodger" Ciara mooned and groaned as he got out the bed to shower, and get ready for is meeting with his gang members. Listen babe, keep the fire burning for me till I get back. You know your my one and only. Only you can make my toes curl, when we do the wild thing Ha..ha, Rodger you are bugging out, but I love you too, and I will keep it hot just for you. Rodger rushed to the shower, as he laughed. He knew deep inside his plan was coming together, one girl at a time. Ciara yelled, "Rodger I do have to go out to pay your phone bill and pick up some groceries. I have a surprise for you, when you come back home. Rodger yelled back, "sounds like a plan, looks like we will be locked down for the entire night."

CHAPTER 3

OLD SCHOOL
VS
NEW SCHOOL

On the West side

Rodger was in the middle of a gang meeting when his phone kept ringing back to back. Everyone looked at him strange, as he excused himself from the meeting to take the call. Yeah Karen, what is it now? This better be good. Hey baby, I just wanted you to know the RRG Crew was up in your unisex snooping around with the first lady of that crew. They were trying to get information on your where a bouts, and how you make yo money. "You know, tryna set you up and rob you!"

"My money," Rodger screamed! Leave the shop go pick up our son, and meet me at my crib. Lay low till I get their.

Ok baby I love you. I love you too, lil mamma.

Rodger began walking slowly back to the meeting angry as ever, this meeting is over. This time next week, I will continue. Is everything ok, G? Everything is everything. Rodger thought to himself, how could this be? I am marring his daughter in a week, and he seemed to finally get the picture that we love each other. Maybe the old man was serious, when he said over his dead body. Then if he is looking for me, I am going to look for him as well. He is going to find out that I will succeed at all cost.

As Rodger thought to himself how to get back at this family, all he heard in his head where the words Mr. Coleman said; "Over my dead body!" Rodger's light-bulb went off in his head, he thought to himself. "I must cut off the head, to make the body weak." Rodger took his time to plan out his next move, knowing the next move he made can be a matter of life and death. No one, especially Symirah can find out my secret plan for destroying the Coleman Family, once and for all. I am going to make my call Rodger stated.

THE BEEF

ing! Ring! Ring! Ring! In a tired voice, RaQuan answered the phone and to his surprise it was Rodger. Yes, your the man I wanted to speak with. "Ok, speak," Ra replied. Well I heard we got beef, and you and yo people need to come to my turf and peace it up, or lay down. RaQuan immediately jumped out and out of bed with great concern. Little boy, are you calling me and my crew out to your part of town? You know little boys should not play with matches it causes fires. Old school, you ain't got no more stain. We The MB Crew run the West and the East, so if you feel frogy, then leap! You know where I be...click.

As Rah sat there and listened to a dial tone, Basimah woke up asking was everything alright. Yeah baby, go back to sleep and don't wake the kids. Well, who was that on the phone no one baby? Now Ra, you wouldn't lye to me right baby? Honey, when T-Mac and Madd Dog brought you home tonight I gave you your pill that forgot to take this morning. Didn't everything work out after that? Yes, your my best friend and I have never keep anything from you right? Yes. So when I say everything is alright, it really is shush… or the kids will be at our door… goodnight. As I kissed my queen on her forehead goodnight.

I am going to call an emergency meeting in the morning. I can't let my family find out about this beef, no matter what the out come. "Symirah!" Girl please keep it down for mom and dad hear you. I can't help if I am in love with my man, and you and A-Boogie aren't getting along lately don't be jealous. Jealous, uh jealous of what; some giggly conversation that is meaningless. Uh, that ain't nothing to run home and tell momma, keep it down I have to go to work in the morning and so do you. Ok Rodger, I can take the day off. Take the day off, so who is going to cover your part tomorrow? Don't worry mom can. No, she can't the doctor needs to meet with her to change her meds. Remember, we almost lost her again.

THE FORBIDDEN ACT
OF PASSION

Dear Diary,

Well, today is a special day; it is August 14, 1995 and today will be the first time for Rodger and I know my parents won't be happy to know that I could not wait till I got married, but the wedding is in a week and I can't wait no longer. I have been thinking what if he can't satisfy me? or if he is big enough for me? Is he going to be the first and last man I ever be with? I am still young and I need

*to make sure it feels right, before I totally commit
to Rodger.*

*I have to test the waters. His conversation is good,
he makes me laugh, but life has many more twist
and turns in it will he be the provider like my Dad
is? Will he protect me like my Dad has? Diary, I
think I am getting cold feet. Its too late my deposits
are on the church, the hall, invitations have gone
out, we have been fitted for gowns and tuxedos,
and the caters is complete. Although dad is not in
favor of my choice, looks as if he is coming around.
Well until next time.......*

Rodger, I told my mother I had to go check on the arrangements
of the hall and our honeymoon plans at GV Travel. Oh, so
you started lying to your parents now? What happened to
the honest woman I met. I'm still here and the hotel is so
beautiful, you sure know how to set the mood baby. Enough
talking, let's set a quiet atmosphere shush..As he began to kiss
me, our bodies begin to rub against each other, oh, it feels
like we do belong together. Rodger began undressing me and
I undressed him. Soon we both were naked, while the moon
light hit our bodies while still engaging in a passionate kiss.

This feels too good to be considered bad. This can't be a sin to have sex before we get married I thought to myself...

Hm was the sound I made, as I gently rubbed my hands slowly up and down his muscular back, as he grabbed my voluptuously butt he led me to the hot tub. We just couldn't keep our hands to ourselves. The water was warm and the bubbles filled the tub. The lights were dim, rose petals were spread from the hot tub leading to the bed. There was even chocolate syrup and cherries on the night stand, and my favorite song was laying softly. Oh wow, this is the perfect way to lose my virginity, and I would not have it any other way, thinking to myself what are the cherries for. Anyway, I've died and gone to heaven. Oo baby right their, u huh don't stop as he nibbled none stop on my ear.

Down to my neck down to my breast, and stayed their teasing my nipples as I begged for more. The bubbles felt just as good as Rodger's touch did. I don't know if I was going or coming. So many thoughts and emotions engulfed me. Rodger whispered softly in my ear I love you, and I want you to have my child. I promise you I will take care of you and my seed. I was so hypnotized by his voice. All I could do was say yes, baby anything you want please don't stop. I want you inside of me right now! He got out of the tub first, and turned back to picked me up, and carry me to the bed where he laid me down gently.

He began pouring the chocolate syrup on my breast dripping down to my navel, and lastly down to my vagina. There he stopped and placed the cherries, so that is what the cherries are for I thought to myself. Rodger began to look at me with his sexy dark brown eyes and said softly, "relax and don't tense up ok baby." I whispered back, "I trust you with my whole heart, your my first, my last and my only." He licked me from my breast down to my vagina and stayed there. He has me so open, I thought as I moaned and groaned. This four play was amazing. He gently climbed on top of me as he cuffed his penis in the palm of him hand, and began to stroke it until it was as hard as a rock.

Taking his time to penetrate my wet vagina, I stayed relaxed cause I knew my man would never hurt me. Suddenly, I felt this painful push, but he said don't tense up. So I grabbed the sheets and he kept pretending it felt good, but I was crying inside. I don't like this part, I just want to scream aloud! "Symirah baby it's ok I am almost inside," Rodger said with a concerned voice. I mumbled, "I am just fine keep going don't stop now I love the pain it turns me on." Rodger quickly got aroused by her words, and began to push even harder. Baby Oh yeah, Oh you feel so good nice and tight, but wet and warm. I love you baby, do you love me?

Yes, yes, yes, Rodger I want your baby please come inside of me Oh shit, now that feels so good. I love it, I want to have you all the time. Mm mm baby, I'm about to come right now..... Uh. Oh Shit, Oh Shit I am coming Ah..Oh yeah, Rodger talk that shit to me baby, I am coming too. R....O....D....G....E....R.... it's coming you feel me coming? Oh yeah, baby that wetness is all over my dick, keep it coming. That's my pussy right? Yes all yours. Suddenly silence filled the room, as we both laid there in each others arms. All I could think about was why did I wait so long to have sex. This is what I have been missing; I am complete now. So did you enjoy your first time baby?

Quietly I said "yes, but am I pregnant yet?" Well, I sure think so especially after what we just did. Your going to be my wife in a week, so I know your are not worried. No, I am just tired I guess. As Rodger jumped in the shower. Where you going? I have to make this run and take care of this business deal. Rest up Ok, I will see you when you get back.

Dear Diary   *August 15, 1995*

Well, we did the forbidden act of passion (sex). It was amazing, like I was in heaven. I wish I had given myself to him a lot earlier. We are checked in the Wynn Starr Hotel in the bridal suite with a hot tub, rose petals, chocolate syrup, moon light, what more can I have asked for on this special day. Rodger just completes me.

I just wised my Dad could understand his little girl is all grown up. Getting married August 21, 1995. I am really excited to be a wife and a mother too. I wonder if they will accept I may be a mother real soon. Until next time.........

CHAPTER FOUR

THE SHOOT OUT GONE WRONG

Rodger was late, and Ciara and as Karen were blowing his phone up with one message after another. Looks as if my plan is falling apart, Rodger thought to himself. I know I made the golden goose pregnant. She is my meal ticket. "Ring", "Ring" hello, man its me Zeus, that old school nigga is on the block asking your where abouts. Listen Zeus I'm in route I don't go around looking for trouble, cause I am trouble. Call Karen let her know, I got her. I am still in a meeting, and kiss my son for me while I call Ciara. Good looking out Zeus. Oh yeah, what was the profit today at the salon? $50.000 Rodger What the hell? That's all. Yeah that is the count.

We will see about that too. Peace. Peace Rodger.

As Rodger sat their, he thought to himself. I was never shook about anything, but I find myself trembling inside; this old school niggas threat about his daughter. I am not the type to run from no one or nothing, it is what it will be. Rodger snapped out of it realizing he did not call his women back. "Ciara, baby it's me, Rodger" listen, this meeting is taking longer that I expected. I will be over in the morning. "Ciara replied, in the morning, what!" remember, we had plans and..... Listen, I got you I promise, I love you Ciara. "Do you love me? "Yeah I love you daddy, Ciara replied sadly." No sooner then Rodger can hang up from Ciara's phone call, Symirah beeped in. Rodger knew he could not lye to Symirah, and he had to hurry back to the Wynn Starr Hotel where he left Symirah. Rodger's empire depended on Symirah's money. Once the head of the Coleman family was destroyed, his money is passed down to his children. With a sinister grin Rodger had planned to cut off the head so the body becomes lifeless.

RODGER GETS SHOT

As Rodger approached the block he did not expect all his workers to be off post. He got out of his car and began walking down 130th Street. Out of nowhere, Rodger heard shots. "Pow!" "Pow!" "Pow!" Oh shit I'm hit Rodger screamed as he fell he hit his head, knocking himself unconscious. The shooter walked over to the body and stood over him saying: I hope this nigga is dead I finished him. Ha, a feeling of pleasure engulfed me, As I bust seven more shots in Rodger's limpness body and I took off. As he laid in a pool of blood Rodger's phone kept ringing endlessly.

Finally someone walking by called 911 and answered his phone. Hello Karen said who is this? Well I found this man lying in a pool of blood and I was hoping you would be helpful enough to tell me who this is. I called 911. Karen screamed out, and began to crying, is he alright, we have a child together." Miss, I don't know he is not moving. "Well, where is he." We are on 130th street. I am on my way Karen said as she hung up the phone. Shortly the emergency services arrived at the scene, and his phone rand again. "Hello where is Rodger," Ciara belted loudly. The emergency worker said "so that is his name?" Duh, yes put him on the phone. Miss, I can't are you his wife? No his girlfriend where is he?

What happened? he has been shot and he is not responding. We are on the way to Memorial Hospital. Can you meet us their? Ciara could not keep herself from crying, but got herself together to answer, "I will be there shortly." Symirah was getting worried; it was late and still no Rodger. She had a big knot in her stomach and knew right away something was wrong. Symirah started dialing jails, then hospitals, and finally she found him.

Symirah prepared herself to take the ride to Memorial Hospital. She thought, "what if Ciara was their? Will she confront me?" Hmm, I will still conduct myself as a lady. My families name is everything and I refuse to step down to a lower level. Symirah noticed a few familiar cars in the parking lot. Symirah began walking slowly to the front door, she braced herself not sure who was inside waiting for her.

ALL OF THE WOMEN MEET

emorial Hospital was filled with the MB Crew. In between the crowded waiting room was his women, Karen, Ciara and Symirah. Karen was rolling her eyes, she knew Symirah.

It is funny Symyirah only knew Ciara, and was very confused why she was their. Ciara remembered her promise to her long time ex-friend. Ciara thought, "I have a blade in my pocket now is the time to cut that bitch." As Ciara started walking closer. Haneefa and Rashidah both walked up to Ciara and said, "if you even think about it you will join Rodger." I got it; I just wanted to become friends again that is all. When Karen saw that from across the room, she changed her mind about confronting Symirah today. Symirah stood strong just thinking, who would do this to my man. I have my own crew, so it will be a war when I find out the details.

"Hey girl, are you ok Ciara," asked Symirah while walking up to her. "Excuse me, I just wanted to swash all this drama between us," she said in a concerned voice; but her heart was far from that. Symirah just walked away to avoid a scene, while her man was hanging on for his life.

Karen stood there like a deer caught in head lights, so confused because Rodger never mentioned Ciara to her. Karen was dazed in her thoughts of being Rodger's first, best, and last love. Meanwhile, Ciara stood still, in a state of shock as tears rolled heavily down her eyes. Thinking to herself, "he said I was his only love!" He wasn't dealing with Symirah any more. Now Symirah had multiple thoughts, but the one thought that played repetitively touched her. Symirah couldn't shack the cold words of her father, saying over my dead body; Rodger, you will not marry my daughter.

Dr. Goldsmith walked out to speak to the family. He asked for the next of kin, and all three women approached him. Karen said, I'm his babies mother, while Ciara said I am carrying his child. Then Symirah said to put things in order, I am his fiancé and the wedding is in two days. "Please Dr. Goldsmith tell me his condition." Dr. Goldsmith continued to saying Mr. Morgan is on life support, we removed three of the bullets. However, Rodger is still in the woods, I'm so sorry. Zeus spoke out, "well is he going to die!" Dr. Goldsmith replied, his chances are slim about 20% right now the life support is keeping him alive. There was such a grieving silence that filled the room.

A FAMILY THAT PRAYS TOGETHER

Mom and Dad walked in the hospital doors with such concern. I want to say one thing, please everyone stop talking just for a minute. You know all this time, I clearly thought this man came into our lives to steal our daughter. Now, I realize that he was the distraction while the enemy snuck in. His job is to steal and kill.

There is no way, he comes to do good. So while we were focused on Rodger, look at the havoc the enemy had caused. When did we forget to pray? Prayer is how we have been successful in life this far. Taking God out was a mistake, we will not repeat. Everyone grab the hand next to the person you are standing next to, and bow your head.

Oh God, we come to you with repentance in our hearts for we have sinned against you. Please forgive us for forgetting about you. Look on Rodger and everyone who is gathered here. Oh God move like never before. We believe in your report no matter what it may look like your report is final. Do a new thing in the lives of your people gathered here. Amen! Amen everyone said.

By the time the prayer came to an end mostly everyone was in tears. The Coleman Family vowed to always keep God head of the family and rise up Above The Drama.

Watch out for my next short novel Matters of The Heart.

coming soon.